CHIHUAHUAS LIKE CHEESE

Janice Wills Kingsbury

JANICE WILLS KINGSBURY

ACKNOWLEDGMENTS

To Mickey Suriani (VCA) and Ike VanderMyde, Bogie's fans.

In memory of my beloved Beau

Fourteen years ago, Beau was rescued from a puppy mill.

He became the most loyal friend I have ever known.

The good man is the friend of all
living things.

Mahatma Gandhi

Bogie is not your typical Chihuahua. He came from a shelter in South Carolina as a stray. When people tried to adopt him at PetSmart with his foster mom, he clung to her shirt with his sharp nails and cried. After several attempts, his foster mom gave in and told Bogie he could stay. This made Bogie very happy.

Bogie is very friendly and goes up to people for pets. People are surprised he is a Chihuahua. It's difficult to know if Bogie thinks he is a Chihuahua and if he knows his size. He acts like a big dog. His pack mates are shelties and a Border Collie and he seems to copy what they do.

When the family goes for hikes, Bogie goes too. He sniffs things and kicks up dirt with his feet like a big dog. He chews big bones, full size bully sticks, and loves his food. If allowed, Bogie will eat as much as the other dogs.

At the beach, Bogie walks all the way to the pier with the others. This is a long way for his short legs. On the way he stops and eats seafood like the others. Sometimes he falls behind and runs as fast as he can to catch up.

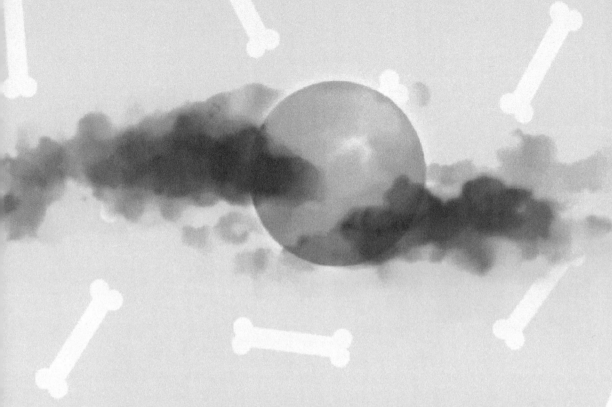

The big Sheltie/Collie, Lexi, likes to sing in the morning and at night before bed. He puts his head in the air and howls two or three syllables. Then the others join in. Bogie sings too. Bogie's song is the loudest and the shrillest of all the dogs.

Even though Bogie thought and acted big, he sometimes felt he didn't get his share of things. One of the bigger dogs always got there first. He was always the last dog to get bones, food, and treats. He was the last dog to get pets on the beach. People didn't see him at first, and they thought he might bite because he is a Chihuahua.

But what bothered him most was he was the last dog to get cheese, his favorite treat in the whole world. By the time he got cheese there would be such a tiny piece left he could barely taste it. This made him cranky and he would grind his teeth, curl his crooked mouth and whine to Ms. J. His whole body would start to wiggle.

He tried new things to get noticed. He stood straight up on his hind legs and danced around, but he was still shorter than the rest of the dogs and got his cheese last.

He stood on the back of the sofa. This made him much higher, but the sofa was too far away from the other dogs and Ms. J almost forgot he was there. Once, he didn't get any cheese at all.

This made Bogie very angry!

He tried jumping on the kitchen table, sitting on the patio chair, bouncing on the bed, and walking across the coffee table. But he was always in the wrong place at the wrong time. When the cheese was handed out, Bogie was always last in line.

Discouraged, he started to take more naps under his blanket.

Bogie liked the sun and often enjoyed lounging in the sun at the beach house in Duck, North Carolina. The sun especially warmed him as the days became chillier.

It was one such day in the beginning of October while he was napping on the deck about to close his big round eyes that he thought he caught the scent of smoke drifting toward him. At the same time he heard a noise close by.

From the deck he could see Cook Drive from beginning to end. And then as he looked across the street he became quite alarmed. The neighbors, Mr. Maynard and Ms. Jane were away. An intruder, with a black hooded jacket was climbing through a side window of their house. He had a big sack in his hand.

This frightened Bogie and he let out his most shrill, ear piercing and Chihuahua sound ever. The sound could be heard all over Duck. It was so loud and shrill that it set off the house alarm.

The house alarm triggered the fire department and the police department who began to sound their alarms also. This woke up Mr. Mark from his afternoon nap. Mr. Mark thought he smelled smoke. He ran out of the house to find that a vacationer had left a burning cigar on the deck when hurrying off to go fishing.

As he ran to the side of the house he saw Ms. Bea's cat had been trapped at the top of the pole on the deck. Kitty had apparently seen the blowing windsock and tried to catch it. Now Kitty was stuck. The dashound next door saw kitty from the third floor deck and was trying to escape to chase him. Mr. Mark quickly called Ron from the Duck Fire Department for help and a ladder!

While Ron hurried to the end of the street with a ladder, he noticed Ms. Stef had slipped and fallen while carrying in her groceries. He worried that she had broken a bone.

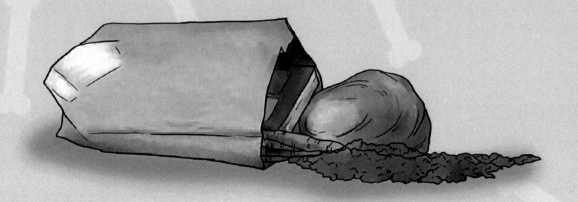

Ms. J, hearing the sirens and alarm, thought the house was on fire and let the Border Collie and other dogs out. Rascal, the wolf dog, happened to be walking by. The pack took off across the street and herded the robber into a corner. He had tried to escape hearing all the noise. Beemer kept him in place while Rascal gave him threatening looks.

Just then three police cars and the fire truck arrived on Cook Drive. Their alarms had gone berserk. They handcuffed the robber and put him in the back of the police car. They took time to thank Bogie and the others and shake hands with Beemer.

Meanwhile the fire truck put out the fire on the deck and gave the vacationer a citation. Another fireman used the ladder on the truck to climb up and rescue kitty and carry the dashund down. They were both scolded and reminded to be careful from now on.

A nice policeman took Ms., Stef to the hospital for a check. She was frightened, but nothing was broken. On their way home, she and the policeman stopped at Duck Donuts for fresh baked, warm, maple glazed donuts and coffee.

Best of all, Bogie got credit for saving the day. It was that fall afternoon in Duck, North Carolina, that a little cheese became a big cheese.

That night Ms. J gave Bogie his cheese first and he got the entire slice to himself.

The mayor wanted to honor Bogie and the others for their service to the community. People applauded Bogie. The Mayor gave him a ribbon and a gift certificate to Outer Banks Cheese Shop.

People stood in line to pet Bogie and give him cheese.

There was a party afterward. There were cheese trays with crackers, cheese stix and cheese dips. There were even cheese curls. Bogie got special gifts from neighbors. Wee Winks gave Bogie a lifetime certificate for free cheese.

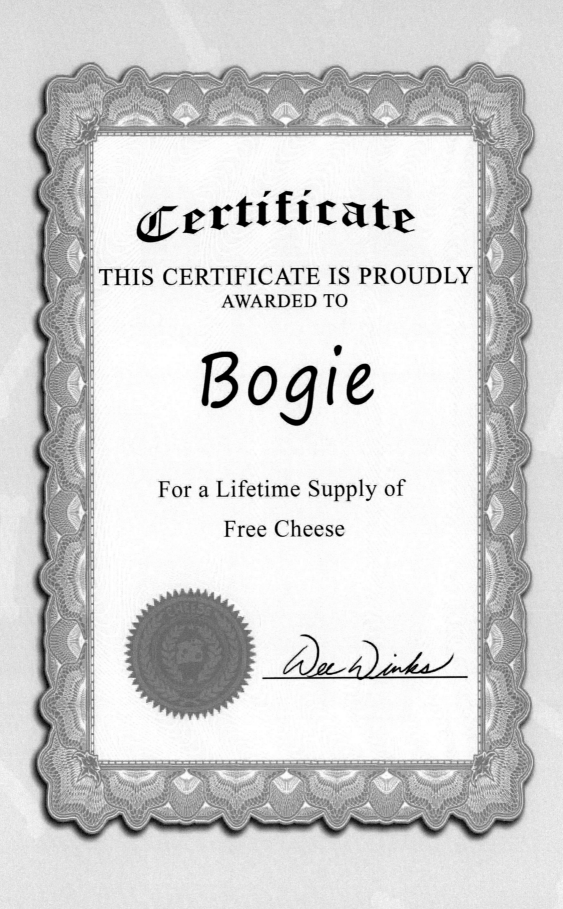

Certificate

THIS CERTIFICATE IS PROUDLY
AWARDED TO

Bogie

For a Lifetime Supply of

Free Cheese

Dee Winks

And suddenly Bogie felt so good from all the praise and attention that he no longer cared so much about cheese. When Petunia came to live with the family she became last in line. Often, Bogie would give her his cheese.

Best of all, Bogie already had the best cheese of all. He had been saved from a shelter and had his own family. He had his own Chihuahua bed and blanket. At night he snuggled up to Ms. J under the covers. What more could any Chihuahua ask?

Bogie learned many
important lessons that week about life:

Size doesn't make you a big cheese

There is always more cheese

There is always someone who wants your
cheese

Give some cheese back to others

Do what you do best and the rest will
work out

ABOUT THE AUTHOR
Janice Wills Kingsbury

If you want more books like Chihuahuas Like Cheese, here are the magic ingredients-
 Mix together:

-1 former school psychologist and teacher

-6 dogs plus fosters

-Lots of beach sand, bright sunny days, and friendly folks, and

-A passion for children, animals, and books,

Dream on the beach in the Outer Banks, create, write, stir, and bake in New Jersey. Store for at least 10 years.

You might also enjoy:
Lexi Goes on Vacation to the Outer Banks

Visit my website for new titles at www.outer-books.com

Bogie lives with his family part time in Mt Laurel, NJ and part time in Duck, NC. He was rescued from a high-kill shelter in South Carolina by Burlington County Animal Alliance. The other dogs in the family, Beau, Lexi, Beemer, Jack, and Hanna are also rescue dogs. Recently Petunia and Potter arrived from North and South Carolina shelters as well. They are great dogs and make people smile wherever they go. Please consider adopting your next pet.

(Left to right: Lexi, Jack, Rascal)

While publishing this book, our beloved friend, Rascal, passed on to The Rainbow Bridge. He was the sweetest wolf dog I have ever met. Many will miss him and Duck Beach will not be the same without him.

Duck Beach, OBX, North Carolina

Made in the USA
San Bernardino, CA
10 May 2015